and sometimes he's very, very clumsy.

Meet some more
of Geoffrey.

His legs are wibbly-wobbly...

and his knees are bendy-buckly...

so he often tangles, trips, skips and flips...

Oh dear, Geoffrey!

Geoffrey bends down as low as he can go
to say hello to the meerkats.

But he slips and slides – and they all disappear in a flash!

Geoffrey won't give up.
He tries to say hello
to the elephants.

But he stumbles,

bumbles

and bumps!

Soon trunks are tangled and tails are tugged…

Oh dear, Geoffrey!

Down at the watering hole, Geoffrey tries to make friends,
but it's very muddy.

He splishes and sploshes...

and then...

SPLASH!

Oh dear, Geoffrey!

Geoffrey is cold and wet and muddy.

He's fed up of being so tall and clumsy.

So he sets off towards his favourite tree –
the tallest one of all, full of tasty
leaves to cheer him up.

"Hello up there!"

On the way, Geoffrey hears a little voice
and feels something tickly.
He looks down to see lots of cheeky
monkeys climbing up his legs!

"You're so tall – please will you help us little ones
up to the top of the tree?" they chatter.

Geoffrey lets them all climb up his long neck.

"Thank you, Geoffrey!" say the monkeys.
"Let's be friends!
We would love to have a friend
as tall as you."

"So would we!"

Geoffrey looks around and notices some little birds…
right under his nose!

"Nobody else can reach up here where we live.
We'd love to be your friends,"
tweet the birds.

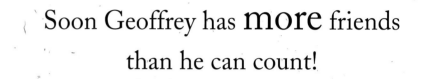

Soon Geoffrey has **more** friends than he can count!

"It's **easy** to make
friends up here!" smiles Geoffrey,
"and I can stretch as high as I like!"

"You're just like us," twitter the birds.
"You can reach as **high** as the sky…

and see as far as the stars!"

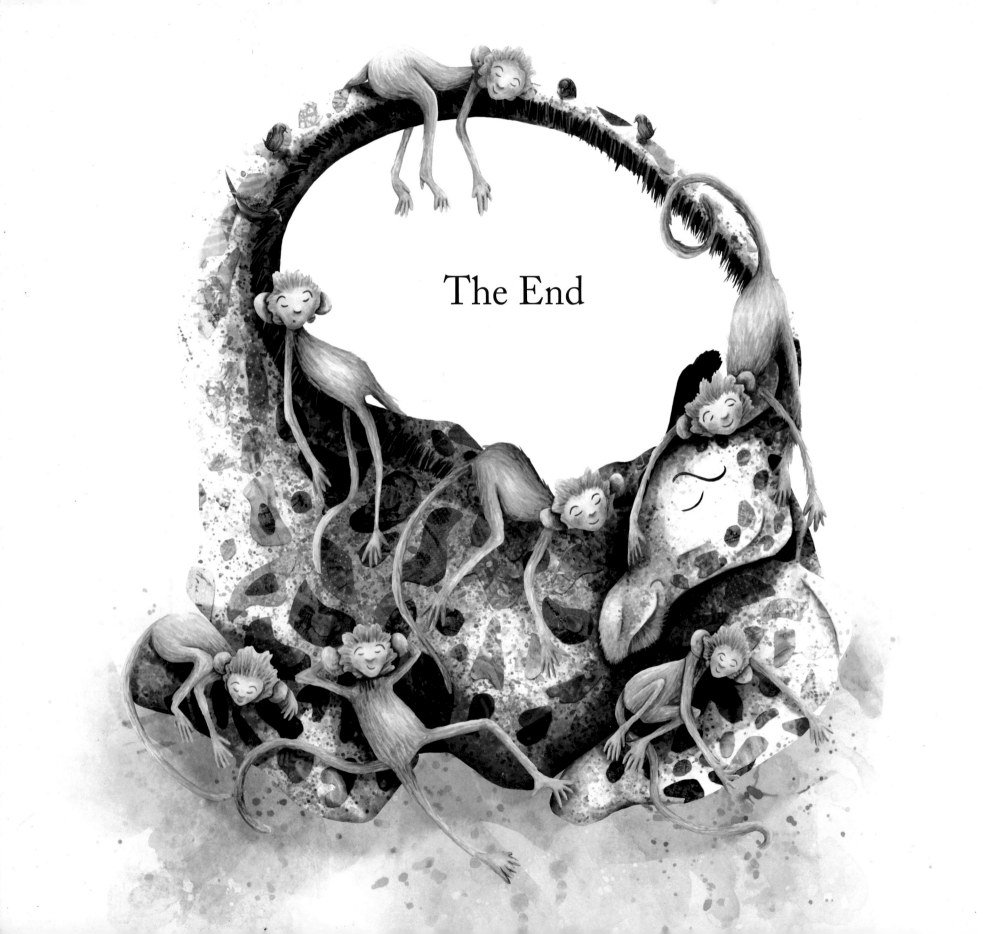

The End